HOW GRANDPA ELF SAVED CHRISTMAS

By Evelyn Gill Hilton

I want to dedicate this little book to my six precious grandchildren, Cameron, Drew, Cassie, Katie, Joshua, and Trenton. May your lives be as blessed and happy as you have made mine with your love and laughter. Meme

Order this book online at www.trafford.com
or email orders@trafford.com

Most Trafford titles are also available at major online book retailers.

Trafford PUBLISHING® www.trafford.com

North America & international
toll-free: 844 688 6899 (USA & Canada)
fax: 812 355 4082

Our mission is to efficiently provide the world's finest, most comprehensive book publishing service, enabling every author to experience success. To find out how to publish your book, your way, and have it available worldwide, visit us online at www.trafford.com

ISBN: 978-1-4269-2151-3 (sc)

Library of Congress Control Number: 2010901382

Print information available on the last page.

Trafford rev. 04/05/2021

The Claus workshop was all abuzz;
Christmastime was close-at-hand.
More children then ever had
Been good throughout the land.

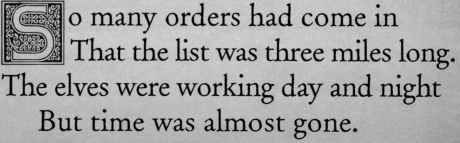

So many orders had come in
That the list was three miles long.
The elves were working day and night
But time was almost gone.

Santa looked at the stacks of toys,
"Christmas Eve's a week away!
How will we get these presents packed
And loaded in the sleigh?"

"The elves are working overtime,"
Kindly answered Mrs. Claus.
"We need more hands to help us, dear,
Or Christmas will be lost!"

So to Elf Town the Clauses went.
"We're as busy as can be;
We need the help of every elf
In our community."

But volunteers were hard to find.
They spent all morning searching.
Bakers baking, teachers teaching,
Every elf was working.

At last they knocked at Grandpa Elf's.
"Sir, our orders have increased.
Although you long ago retired,
We need your expertise."

"You hold the North Pole record as
Fastest packer in the land."
"By Jimminy," laughed Grandpa Elf,
"I'll give those squirts a hand!"

Grandpa was so excited, he
Left his glasses on the shelf.
He entered the workshop shouting,
"The Champ is here to help!"

"Hmmm, let me see," he read the list,
All this writing is so small…
A truck for Chloe, jacks for Beau,
A book for Baby Paul."

With lightning speed he packed the gifts
And he very soon was through.
Grandpa had mixed up all the names
But no one even knew.

While Mrs. Claus brought Santa's coat,
The Elves loaded up the sleigh.
Then they all saluted Grandpa,
"Hurrah, you saved the day!"

The reindeer shook their harness bells
And eagerly pawed the snow.
Saint Nick checked the radar screen, then
Called, "Giddy-Up, Let's Go!"

Slowly, faster, then Wh-o-o-osh! Airborne!
Up into the great jet stream
Zoomed the big Claus Company Sleigh
And Santa's magic team.

As they approached the speed of light,
The dual stardust exhaust
Cast a beautiful brilliance on
Earth's silvery midnight frost.

ittle Drew looked out his window
Up into the midnight sky.
He gazed wide-eyed as Santa's sleigh
And team came flying by.

Deep down inside the big toy sack
Dolly whispered to Teddy,
"I'm really meant for Jaci and
You are meant for Freddy."

Around the world, quick as a wink,
All the toys were delivered.
But heading home Santa worried,
"Something's wrong," he shivered.

On Christmas Morning helpers called
With news from far and near.
Gifts were mixed up from Maine to France.
Grandpa goofed, it was clear!

"Our reputation's ruined," cried
The little elves in horror!
"The children must be very sad,"
Santa sighed in sorrow.

Old Grandpa Elf felt very bad,
So he packed to move away;
He knew he had ruined Christmas
And now he could not stay.

Then Post Elf brought in stacks of mail
To everyone's great surprise,
Happy girls and boys had written—
Six million cards arrived!

In wonder, Santa stroked his beard.
All the children loved their toys.
Boys got presents they'd never had
And girls liked toys for boys!

MiLing liked Juan's piñata.
Blake liked Kenta's jungle drum.
Everyone thought this year's gifts
Were very dandy ones!

Sean and Cassie traded gifts.
Others kept them just for fun.
New friendships all around the world,
Because of Grandpa, had begun.

Young Cameron's rocking baby dolls.
Gabby's building model planes.
Mrs. Claus laughed until she cried,
"Oh my, how times have changed!"

Katie laughed and traded her tool kit
For Josh's yarn and skirt.
But Grammy unwrapped Trent's long board
And headed for the surf!

ld Grandpa blushed and stammered when
Elves cheered in unison, "I'd
Have read the names right if I'd tried—
I switched them just for fun!"

ow if you get a present that's
Meant for Mom, Dad, or a friend,
You'll know that dear old Grandpa Elf
Is helping Santa

Once
Again!

Printed in the United States
by Baker & Taylor Publisher Services